Too Loud!!!!!!!

by Karen Szybalski

Dedication:

My deepest appreciation goes to my husband, Peter, and son, Bryan, Hackett for their encouragement and support.

To my parents, Joanne and Carl Szybalski, and my sister, Annette Szybalski. To the entire Hackett clan. Thank you all for being in my life!

To my critique group partners, Lucy Geever-Conroy, Gail Ishimatsu, Suzanne Morrone and Emily Chiang.

"Too Loud"
by Karen Szybalski
Originally published in 2003

"Too Loud," was originally published on the weeonesmag.com website in 2003.

The lawn mower roars.

MMRROOWWW MMRROOWWW MMRROOWWW

MMRROOWWW MMRROOWWW MMRROOWW

MMRROOWWW MMRROOWWW

"Stop, that noise."

The dog barks.

"Ouch, my ears!"

The hairdryer buzzes.

“Too loud!”

The baby cries.

The vacuum cleaner vibrates.

“Turn that off.”

The toilet swishes.

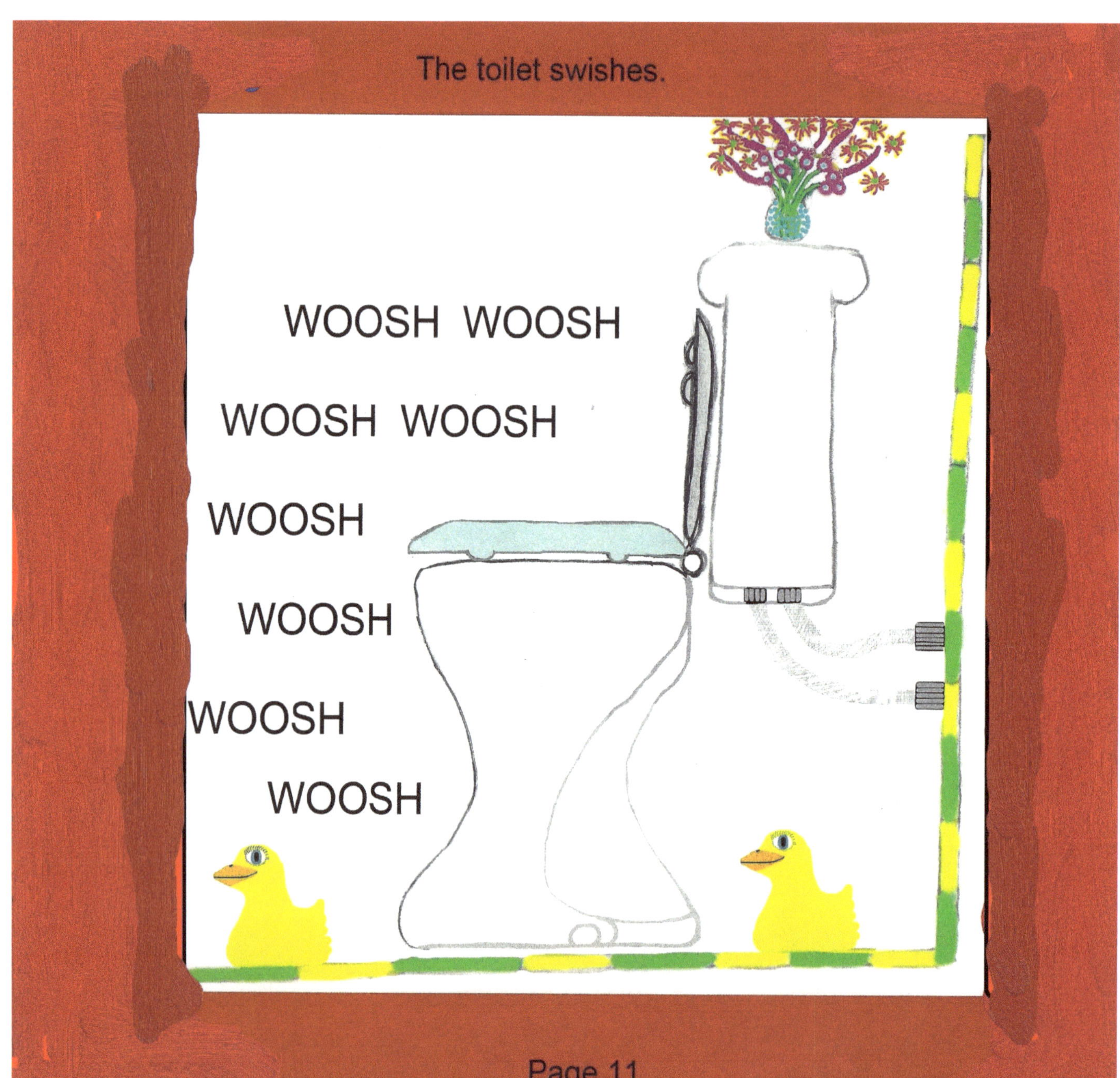

"Too, much noise."

The jackhammer breaks the road.

"Too, noisy."

"It's so quiet!

haaaa, haaaaa, haaaa
haaaa, haaaaaaa,
haaaaaaaaaa,
haaaaaaaaaaaa,
haaaaaaaa

ppeeee, yippeee, yippeee, yipp
eee, yippeee, yippeee, yippeee
eee, yippeee, yippeee, yippee
eee, yippeee, yippeee, yippee
yippeee, yippeee, yippee

"Quiet down in there!"

"Oh, nooooooooooooo!"

The lightening explodes.

"Ouch, my ears!"

The police car whines.

"Too loud!"

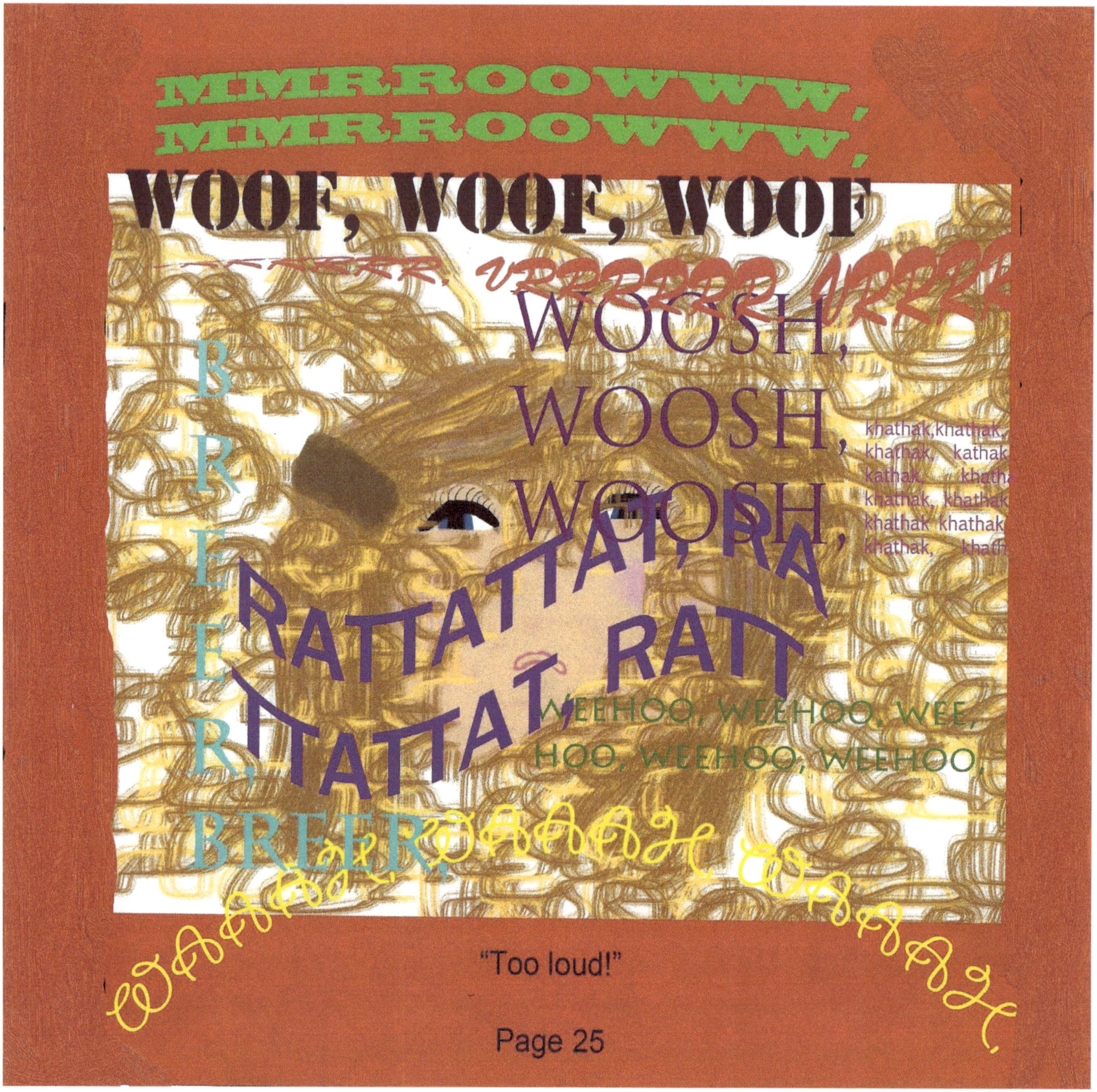

MMRROOWWW,
MMRROOWWW,
WOOF, WOOF, WOOF
VRRR, VRRRRRR VRRRR
WOOSH, WOOSH, WOOSH,
khathak,khathak, khathak, kathak kathak, khatha khathak, khathak khathak khathak khathak, khath
BREER, BREER,
RATTATTAT, RA
TATTAT, RATT
WEEHOO, WEEHOO, WEE, HOO, WEEHOO, WEEHOO,
WAAAH, WAAAH, WAAAH,

"Too loud!"

"Oh, well. I might as well join in."

ABOUT THE AUTHOR

Karen Szybalski is a published story, song, and poem writer. Her playful use of color, language, and music bring her stories to life with cheerful audience participation. She lives in Northern California with her husband, Peter, son, Bryan, dog, and cat.

Geared towards younger children and anyone who lives with sound over-load.

Karen Szybalski is a published story, poem, play, and song writer.
Visit my website:
http://www.karenszybalski.blogspot.com

www.ingramcontent.com/pod-product-compliance
Lightning Source LLC
LaVergne TN
LVHW071215160826
845679LV00003B/833
9798374917260